Emily's Secret

Emily leaned forward and lowered her voice. "Do you remember when my father caught his bare foot in the wheel of his bike and the spokes cut off his toe?"

Everyone remembered.

"Well," continued Emily, "nobody could find the toe in time to stick it back on his foot." She paused dramatically. "I never told anybody about this—not even my parents. But the next day I went back to the place where he had the accident. And I looked all over for his lost toe."

No one dared ask what everyone was thinking.

Finally Billy said in a hushed voice, "Did you find it?"

Emily nodded solemnly.

Tulu gasped.

"Cool!" said Spike.

"Nasty!" squealed Frankie.

"So what did you do?" asked Billy, his dark eyes shining with curiosity.

"I saved it," whispered Emily. "In a matchbox."

"Sims's characteristically appealing pencil illustrations add to the humor in this funny, first chapter book."
—*School Library Journal*

A CANAL STREET KIDS BOOK

THE WORLD'S GREATEST TOE SHOW

A CANAL STREET KIDS BOOK

THE WORLD'S GREATEST TOE SHOW

by Nancy Lamb and Muff Singer

illustrated by Blanche Sims

little rainbow®

Troll Associates

Published by Troll Associates, Inc.
Little Rainbow is a trademark of Troll Associates.

First published in hardcover by BridgeWater Books.

Printed in the United States of America.

10 9 8 7 6 5 4 3 2 1

Library of Congress Cataloging-in-Publication Data

Lamb, Nancy.
The world's greatest toe show / by Nancy Lamb and Muff Singer.
p. cm.
Summary: The five Canal Street Kids are certain that their unusual
booth at the school fair will bring in the most money and win them
the grand prize.
ISBN 0-8167-3322-8 (lib.) ISBN 0-8167-3323-6 (pbk.)
[1. Fairs—Fiction. 2. Schools—Fiction. 3. Toes—Fiction.]
I. Singer, Muff. II. Title.
PZ7.L16725Wo 1994
[Fic]—dc20   93-28440

CHAPTER ONE

The Canal Street Club wouldn't have caused so much trouble if Emily Anderson hadn't saved her father's toe in a matchbox.

Or if Frankie Stevens hadn't wanted to be a famous movie extra. Or if Bunny Bigalow and Violetta Epstein hadn't been so obnoxious.

Everyone knew Frankie was dying to be a movie star. And everyone knew about Bunny and Violetta, too. But no one knew about the matchbox or Mr. Anderson's toe. That was Emily's secret.

It probably should have stayed a secret, Emily thought after the disaster at the Spring Fair. But by then, it was too late.

Emily hadn't expected trouble when Mr. Bottoms, the principal of Washington Elementary, announced the plan for the kids-only school fair.

After Mr. Bottoms described the Grand Prize for the booth that raised the most money at the fair, Emily Anderson's best girlfriend, Frankie Stevens, called an emergency meeting of the Canal Street Club. All the club members were in fifth grade, except for Frankie's little sister, Tulu, who was a junior member because she was only in first grade.

That afternoon, the five Canal Street Club members gathered in the clubhouse they had fixed up in Spike Piranna's attic. Spike lived with his grandparents, who were both hard of hearing. So they didn't mind the noise the kids made during their club meetings.

"If we win the Grand Prize at the Spring Fair," Frankie said as soon as she called the meeting to order, "it's our big chance to be rich and famous!"

"Being an extra in a movie won't make us rich or famous," Billy Lopez said. Billy knew a lot about movies. His father worked for one of the movie studios. Mr. Lopez created special effects, like flying brooms and scary monsters that ooze globs of gore.

"Well, being an extra will make us more rich and famous than we are right now," said Emily as she poked the large scab on her elbow.

"Just think of it," Frankie continued, tossing her long blond hair to one side. "If the Canal Street Club puts together the booth that makes the most money, we can win the Grand Prize and be extras in a *real* Hollywood movie!"

"Yes!" said Tulu, jumping up in excitement. Then she leaned over and whispered in Frankie's ear, "What's an extra?"

Frankie rolled her green eyes dramatically. "Extras are extra people in movies," she explained to her little sister. "They get to hang out in the background, like all the kids on bicycles in *E.T.*"

"So?" said Spike Piranna. "What's the big deal? Extras aren't even allowed to talk."

"A career has to start somewhere," answered Frankie. She had wanted to be a movie star ever since the day she met Miss Piggy at a shopping mall.

Everybody in the whole school would see us, Emily thought. Especially Bunny Bigalow and Violetta Epstein. "I think being in a movie would be wonderful," she said.

"Emily's right," said Frankie in her official club president voice. "Everyone in favor of making the most fantastic booth at the school fair and winning the Grand Prize, raise your hand."

Everyone voted yes.

"What kind of booth should we have?" asked Spike, chewing on a large wad of bubble gum. "My grandmother can read palms."

Frankie shook her head. "Noah Benchley's group has signed up for a fortune-telling booth," she said. "They've got a Ouija board and an Eight-ball table already planned. I copied the list of booths that have been taken so far. There's a paint–your–own–T-shirt booth, a ring toss, and a face-decorating booth. And some second-grade girls are doing a handicrafts booth."

"We could bake cookies and things," interrupted Tulu. Her real name was Louisa, but her sister called her Tagalong Tulu. And the name stuck. "I could make cupcakes with sprinkles," she added.

"Bunny Bigalow and Violetta Epstein are planning a bake sale booth," said Frankie.

"Yuck!" said Emily and Spike.

Billy Lopez groaned.

"Have you ever tasted Mrs. Epstein's carob bran brownies?" asked Emily. "They taste like chocolate dog food."

"They're not as bad as her cheeseless tofu

cheesecake," said Spike. "Totally gross," he added, sticking his finger in his mouth.

"Wouldn't you bake gross food if you had Violetta for a daughter?" Billy asked.

"I'd bake *Violetta* if I had her for a daughter," said Emily. "She and Bunny Bigalow are the most stuck-up girls in the whole fifth grade. There's nothing they'd like better than bragging to everyone about beating us out for the Grand Prize. The thought of those two show-offs being in the movie instead of us makes me sick."

"The trouble is, everybody likes bake sales." Billy sighed. "I bet Bunny and Violetta will make tons of money. We'll never beat them."

"You always give up so easily," Frankie snapped. "Of course we can beat them. We *have* to."

"Besides," said Emily, "if those two girls win, they'll be even more obnoxious than they already are. They'll laugh us out of school." She could just imagine how they'd brag.

"So how can we beat them?" asked Spike.

"We'll beat them by doing something unusual," said Frankie in her super-dramatic stage voice. "All those booths we named are regular kinds of things, even the bake sale booth. We need something different. Something to attract lots of customers. Something new or weird or gross."

Emily looked at Spike. Anything gross appealed to him. But Spike looked right back at Emily and shrugged.

Everyone looked at everyone else. Not one member of the Canal Street Club had a new idea. Emily twiddled her thumbs. Spike Piranna blew a gigantic bubble that stuck in his eyebrows when it popped, and Tulu fidgeted with her pigtails.

"Come on, gang!" Frankie urged. "Or we'll be watching Bunny and Violetta signing autographs after the movie premiere. Think of something fantastic or we can kiss our movie star dreams good-bye."

"Maybe we could have a cockroach contest," suggested Billy. "I've got a gigantic, two-inch specimen. A sure winner."

Frankie shook her head. "I don't think Mr. Bottoms would allow cockroaches all over the school," she said. "But thanks, anyway."

Should I tell them? thought Emily, casually checking out the bruise on her elbow. Why not? "I have an idea that's never been done," she said.

"What?" asked Spike.

Everyone leaned forward expectantly.

"What about…" Emily stopped and shook her head. Her short red curls bounced like copper Slinkys. Everyone will think I'm crazy, she thought. "Nah…it's just too weird."

"*What* is?" the gang demanded.

Frankie reached over and poked Emily. "Come on! Tell us."

"Well…nah…you'll think it's too gross."

Spike's eyes lit up. "*Too* gross?"

"Come on, Emily!" added Tulu.

"Okay." Emily nodded. She took a deep breath. "What about a toe show?" she asked. "It would be totally new, totally weird, and totally gross, too."

"Huh?" said Frankie.

"A toe show," repeated Emily.

"You mean, like dancing?" asked Tulu.

"No. This has nothing to do with dancing," Emily said. She leaned forward and lowered her voice. "Do you remember when my father caught his bare foot in the wheel of his bike and the spokes cut off his toe?"

Everyone remembered.

"Well," continued Emily, "nobody could

find the toe in time to stick it back on his foot."
She paused dramatically. "I never told anybody
about this—not even my parents. But the next
day I went back to the place where he had the
accident. And I looked all over for his lost toe."

No one dared ask what everyone was
thinking.

Finally Billy said in a hushed voice, "Did
you find it?"

Emily nodded solemnly.

Tulu gasped.

"Cool!" said Spike.

"Nasty!" squealed Frankie. Wide-eyed, she
turned to Emily. "Do you actually mean to tell
us that you went back to the scene of the
accident and rescued your father's toe?"

"Uh-huh," replied Emily.

"You mean you picked it up?" asked
Frankie. "With your bare hands?"

"Of course. What was I going to do? I
couldn't just leave it there. That wouldn't have
been polite. And I couldn't throw it in the trash."

"So what did you do?" asked Billy, his dark
eyes shining with curiosity.

"I saved it," whispered Emily. "In a
matchbox."

CHAPTER TWO

Everyone in the attic froze. Only the drone of a plane overhead interrupted the silence as each kid tried to imagine exactly what a toe in a matchbox looked like.

Suddenly Spike popped a giant bubble and everyone jumped.

"Can we see it?" asked Billy, who wondered whether the toe would be interesting or disgusting.

"Sure," said Emily. "It's in my room. But remember, it's a secret."

"Let's go!" said Spike, heading for the door.

One by one, the five club members climbed down the attic ladder and ran outside. Emily made a running, one-legged jump onto her skateboard. Perfect execution, she thought. She led the way as the gang raced down the sidewalk to her house at the end of Canal Street.

"What's going on?" asked Mrs. Anderson as the kids burst through her front door, with Tulu tagging along at the rear.

"Nothing!" called Emily as she bolted up the stairs, followed by the other club members.

As soon as all the kids were in Emily's room, she closed the door. Immediately everyone grew quiet.

"Where is it?" whispered Spike, glancing around the room.

"Over there." Emily pointed to her bed.

"You sleep with a toe?" shrieked Frankie.

"Don't be silly," Emily said. "It's *under* the bed."

"Creepy," said Frankie with a shiver.

"Gross," said Spike with a grin.

Emily lay down on her stomach and reached under the bed to her hiding place. Slowly she pulled out the matchbox and sat up.

"Here it is," she announced, feeling very important.

Nobody moved. Nobody said a word.

"Well, don't you want to see it?" Emily asked.

Spike swallowed. "S-sure," he said.

Sitting with her back to her bed, Emily placed the matchbox in front of her. The other kids inched closer. Slowly, reverently, Emily pushed the inside box out of its cover.

Holding their breaths, her friends looked in the box.

"It looks like a wad of cotton," Tulu said.

"It *is* a wad of cotton," said Emily. "You didn't think I was going to let my father's toe roll all over the place, did you?"

"Of course not," Tulu said politely.

Frankie squirmed nervously.

"So what's it look like?" asked Spike.

Emily held out the box, lifted up the cotton and then sang out, "Ta-da!"

Tulu squealed and scrunched her eyes shut.

"That's a toe?" whispered Billy.

"Nasty!" Spike pronounced as he stared at something that looked like a yellowish brown prune with a gray toenail.

"It's weird, all right," said Billy, slowly shaking his head.

"It's different, all right," said Frankie.

Tulu nodded. "Yep," she managed to squeak.

"I can see it now," Frankie said. "Everybody in the school will want to see your father's

toe. We'll make more money than anybody else. We'll leave Bunny Bigalow and Violetta Epstein in the dust! We'll make more money than anybody in the history of Washington Elementary School. I *know* we will. This sensational, show-stopping toe is a guaranteed sure winner!"

Emily beamed with pride. It *is* a sure winner, she thought.

"So what should we charge for admission?" asked Billy.

"Five cents a peek," said Tulu.

"No, that's not nearly enough," said Frankie. "We'll never make the most money if we charge just a nickel."

"How about a dollar a customer?" suggested Spike.

"Too much," Frankie said.

"I've got it!" said Emily. "Fifty cents a peek. How's that?"

"And seventy-five cents a touch," Frankie added.

Tulu shivered.

"At least seventy-five," Spike agreed.

"The money's settled then," Frankie said.

"What we have to figure out now is what to call our booth," said Billy.

"That's easy," said Frankie, jumping up. "Can't you just hear it?" She spread her arms dramatically. "Come and see it, ladies and gentlemen! Come and touch it, folks! This is a once-in-a-lifetime opportunity. Now, for a limited time only, you can see The World's Greatest Toe Show!"

CHAPTER THREE

The next day at school, Emily walked behind Ms. Nelson and Mr. Yang on the way to the lunchroom. They were the teachers supervising the Spring Fair.

"It was a great idea to let the students organize the fair this year!" Emily heard Ms. Nelson say. "Did you see how many groups have already signed up for booths?"

"I did," said Mr. Yang. "Having the children choose and design their own booths was a terrific idea."

"It looks like we've got a big success on our hands," said Ms. Nelson.

"By the way," said Mr. Yang, "what's a toe show?"

Oops! thought Emily, holding her breath.

"Hmmm. Must be some kind of a dance," said Ms. Nelson, shrugging her shoulders.

Whew! Emily exhaled.

"Sounds original," said Mr. Yang, as he and Ms. Nelson went to sit at the teachers' table.

You don't know *how* original, Emily said to herself, looking around the lunchroom for Frankie so they could sit together.

By the end of the week, every kid in school knew that the Canal Street Club was having a toe show at the Spring Fair.

"What's a toe show?" Noah Benchley asked Frankie and Emily at recess.

"It's probably a silly dance or something," said Ben Henderson.

"It's a secret." Frankie smiled. "You'll have to pay fifty cents to find out."

"I think they're going to paint funny pictures on our feet," said Jade Singer.

"Maybe it's a contest to see who has the longest second toe," said Genevieve Tuttle.

"Whatever it is, a toe booth can't possibly make as much money as *our* booth," Violetta Epstein said smugly.

"Of course not," agreed Bunny Bigalow.

"That's what *you* think," Emily said, glaring at the two girls. "I bet you each a dollar that our booth wins. When we're rich and famous movie stars, a dollar won't mean anything."

Bunny sneered, "That's the easiest money I'll ever make. It's a bet."

"Me, too," said Violetta. "It'll be as easy as taking candy from a baby."

Her teeth gritted, Emily shook hands with her two worst enemies. Just you wait, she thought.

The idea of those two winning one more thing made Emily shudder. They were terrible winners—the worst, Emily added to herself. When Bunny won the fifth-grade spelling bee, she wore her blue ribbon to school every day. Even to gym. And every time anybody asked her a question, she spelled out the answer.

Violetta was just as bad. In kindergarten, she actually put up campaign signs to be elected captain of toilet recess. And when she won, she let all the kids who had voted for her go first in line. Even when Emily was about to wet her pants, Violetta just smiled and said, "Wait your turn. Wait your turn. I'm the captain."

Emily clenched her fist. No matter what, she

vowed, we're going to win that Grand Prize.

For days, all the kids at Washington Elementary talked about the toe show. But no matter what anybody said, no matter what anybody guessed, the Canal Street Club kept the secret. Absolutely nobody, they had decided, *nobody* was allowed to know what the toe show was about until the day of the Spring Fair. Until they had paid their money. Until they had seen the toe.

"And even then," said Emily, "we have to make them promise they won't tell anyone about the show. That way, every kid in school will still pay to find out what a toe show is."

"What if grown-ups want to come into our booth?" asked Tulu. "They might tell about..." She lowered her voice. "...the dead toe."

"Grown-ups are just supposed to supervise," replied Emily. "It's a kids-only fair, and that means only kids can come into our booth."

"Or any of the other booths," added Spike.

"We'll have the most popular booth at the Spring Fair!" Frankie exclaimed. "I know we will. I can already see my name in lights!"

As the day of the Spring Fair drew closer,

the Canal Street Club members were busy with final arrangements for their booth.

Emily covered the matchbox with black velvet. She decorated the top with rhinestones glued in the shape of a glittering bicycle wheel. Elegant, she thought.

Frankie painted signs that read COME SEE THE WORLD'S GREATEST TOE SHOW. And Spike and Billy posted the signs all over the neighborhood. Tulu held the tape for them.

Spike was in charge of writing out the promise the kids had to make when they entered the toe show.

Billy and Emily built a wooden frame for the booth. Billy's dad helped. They were going to hang sheets all the way around the frame. That way, the customers could step inside the booth, and each viewing would be private.

"What is this toe show, anyway?" asked Mr. Lopez when they were working on the booth. "Some kind of dance?"

"Not exactly," Billy answered. "Where do you want me to hammer this nail?"

The day before the fair, Frankie called a special meeting of the Canal Street Club to

discuss the last-minute details for the booth. All
the kids met in Spike's attic after school.

"Okay," said Frankie. "I'm calling this
meeting to order."

Everyone quieted down.

"I've made a list of jobs for the fair. To begin
with, it's only right for Emily to be the toe
holder. She'll sit behind the table and hold on to
the toe box during the viewings."

"Right," the others agreed.

"Who's going to collect the money?"
Frankie continued.

"Billy could do that," Emily said.

"Good," said Frankie. Then she looked at
Spike. "You'll be the one to read the promise the
kids have to make before they enter the booth."

"A promise that serious is called an oath,"
Billy said.

Spike nodded.

"No promise, no peek," Emily said.

"I want to be the curtain puller," Tulu piped
up excitedly.

"Okay," Frankie said, writing Tulu's name in
her notebook. "Curtain puller it is." She turned
to Spike. "You'll have to be the bodyguard, too."

"What do I do?" he asked.

"You check tickets and make sure people don't touch the toe unless they pay full price. And you also have to take care of any trouble that might come up."

Good choice, thought Emily. Spike's the biggest kid in the class.

"I'm going to be the announcer," Frankie said in her movie-star voice. "It'll be good practice for my career." She paused. "Have I left out anything for us to do?"

"My dad will set up the frame for the booth later this afternoon," Billy said, playing with his pet caterpillar as it crawled over the top of his fingers and hand.

"Perfect," said Frankie.

"Where should we meet?" asked Emily.

"We'll meet here at eight o'clock tomorrow morning, and we'll walk over to school together. Then we'll get ready for The World's Greatest Toe Show." Frankie closed her notebook.

The five kids stood in a circle. They held their left arms out toward the center and grasped each other's hands. They pumped their arms up and down three times.

"Canal Street Forever!" they all called out. It was their club motto. "Forever and Ever!"

CHAPTER FOUR

Spike Piranna's grandmother read palms and horoscopes and tea leaves. She could have told the club that there was trouble ahead at the Spring Fair. But nobody asked her.

Emily and the other kids weren't expecting trouble. The sun was shining, the weather was warm, and there wasn't a cloud in the sky. They met at the clubhouse as planned.

"Emily, do you have the toe?" Frankie asked.

Emily held up a brown paper lunch bag with the toe box inside. "Right here," she said.

"I've got the banner," said Billy.

Frankie consulted her list. "Did everyone remember to bring a sheet?"

All the kids held up folded squares of material.

"Great!" exclaimed Frankie. "Then let's

move it and get this show on the road!"

Just as the group reached the corner, a woman's voice called out, "Francesca! Louisa! Wait for me! Where's my good-bye kees?" The voice spoke in a heavy French accent. Mrs. Stevens, Frankie and Tulu's mother, was from Paris, France.

"Oh, no," moaned Frankie. She glanced at Tulu. "Why couldn't we have been born with a regular mother?"

"I thought she *was* regular," said Tulu.

"Spare me," mumbled Frankie, whose mother insisted on calling her by her real name, Francesca.

Mrs. Stevens's flowing scarves floated behind her as she ran up beside her two daughters. She bent over and kissed Tulu. Then she turned to Frankie.

"Francesca! Ees that leep-steek you are wearing?" she asked.

"Yes, it is lipstick," Frankie said with a big sigh. "It's makeup for the show."

"Ah, yes," said Mrs. Stevens. "I guess it ees all right for you to wear leep-steek on the stage."

Frankie rolled her eyes.

"Well, I hope you have a fantasteek show!"

Mrs. Stevens said to everyone with a smile. "As they say in show beesness, break a leg!"

"Huh?" said Spike.

"Don't worry," Frankie explained quickly. "It's just a superstitious saying that means good luck. We actors and actresses use it all the time."

"What a weird way to say something nice," commented Billy as the gang started down the street toward the playground of Washington Elementary School.

The bake sale booth was already set up when the Canal Street kids got to the school. A blue and red net ruffle hung all around the table. Bunny and Violetta wore matching blue aprons with red and blue net bows in their hair.

Wouldn't you know, thought Emily.

"Revolting," said Frankie.

Spike ignored the bake sale booth. "Let's get to work," he said.

The frame for the toe booth was set up right in the middle of the playground between the spin art and ring toss booths. The Canal Street Club wasted no time in getting everything ready for the show.

First they climbed up on chairs and started

to hook the sheets onto the nails all the way around the frame.

"Here, let me help you do that," offered Mr. Bottoms, the principal. He hurried over to Spike, who was holding up a Mickey Mouse sheet next to a dinosaur sheet.

"Thanks," said Spike.

Soon the curtains were hung all the way around the frame.

"Time to run," said Mr. Bottoms. "It's a busy day. Good luck. I'll catch your show later."

The kids giggled.

"Dinosaurs, Mickey Mouse, and astronauts?" said Bunny Bigalow in her snootiest voice.

Emily turned and glared at her. "We want our booth to be colorful," she said. "Besides, what's wrong with mix and match?"

"What's wrong is that your mix doesn't match," said Bunny. "Our booth is color coordinated. It's decorated in various shades of periwinkle and cranberry."

"It looks like red and blue to me," said Tulu.

"It is," said Spike, looking right at Bunny and Violetta. "But matching colors don't forecast a winning booth."

"We'll see," Bunny said. She laughed and

shook her head as she skipped back to the blue and red booth.

Emily clenched her teeth. "We certainly *will* see," she muttered, thinking how much fun she'd have collecting her bet.

Spike and Billy hooked the last sheet across the middle of the booth on the inside, making a private viewing room for Emily and the toe. Then they hung the banner over the front of the booth. It was decorated with lots of glittering four-toed footprints and big block letters that spelled out THE WORLD'S GREATEST TOE SHOW.

Frankie and Emily carried two desks out of the sixth-grade classroom. They placed one just outside the booth's entrance and taped a sign on it that read:

```
┌─────────────────────────────────┐
│                                 │
│       ONE PEEK — 50¢            │
│       ONE TOUCH — 75¢           │
│                                 │
└─────────────────────────────────┘
```

Inside the viewing room, Emily covered the other desk with a piece of red satin fabric she had brought from her mother's sewing room. The glittering black velvet box looked elegant

sitting on red satin, she thought as she sat down.

By nine-thirty, the playground was packed. The sounds of kids laughing and calling competed with the whine of the helium machine filling up balloons. Circus music played over loudspeakers, and bubbles from the bubble booth floated overhead. It was a perfect day.

A large crowd gathered around the color-coordinated bake sale booth. Violetta and Bunny pranced back and forth while they cut brownies into squares and poured lemonade for lots of hungry customers. Their periwinkle and cranberry net hair bows fluttered in the soft breeze.

"They're probably making a fortune," Billy said glumly, staring at the bake sale booth.

"But not as much as we will," Spike said with a grin as he looked at the line of kids waiting to see the toe show.

"Such a long line!" exclaimed Mrs. Stevens as she bustled up to the entrance of the booth. "Since I'm the mama of Francesca and Louisa, surely I can go een right now...."

Billy glanced at Frankie, who looked horrified at the thought of her mother seeing Mr. Anderson's toe.

"I'm very sorry, Mrs. Stevens," said Billy in his most adult voice. "Cutting in line isn't fair. And, anyway, this is a kids-only booth."

"I'll come back later when the line ees shorter," she said. "Surely 'kids only' doesn't mean no parents."

Frankie groaned and waited till her mother was out of sight. "Step right up, ladies and gentlemen!" she cried. "Come and see The World's Greatest Toe Show. It'll fascinate you! It'll shock you! It'll thrill you! Don't pass up this once-in-a-lifetime opportunity. Never before! Never again! This is your one and only chance. Step right up, ladies and gentlemen! This is the gen-u-ine article! Step right up!"

One by one, the kids from Washington Elementary stepped right up to the curtain. And one by one, Frankie allowed them inside.

"Are you prepared to take the oath?" Spike asked Noah Benchley when his turn came.

"What oath?"

"The oath of secrecy," Spike said mysteriously.

"I guess so." Noah shrugged.

"Then raise your right hand, please," said Spike, "and repeat after me."

"Cross my eyes and kiss my elbow..."

Spike began.

"Cross my eyes and kiss my elbow..." Noah repeated.

"On my honor, I promise not to reveal to anyone what I see in the toe booth today...."

When Noah finished the oath, Spike asked him, "Do you want to touch it or just take a look at it?"

"Touch what?" asked Noah.

"The toe," said Spike casually.

"That doesn't sound so special," Noah said. "Maybe I don't want to do anything at all."

"Wow!" yelled Ben Henderson from behind the curtain that surrounded Emily's viewing table. "Are you serious?"

Noah stopped and listened. Spike popped another bubble.

"Yes," Emily whispered. "It's the real thing."

"Unbelievable!" Ben cried.

"I'll touch it!" Noah said instantly.

"That'll be seventy-five cents," said Billy.

Outside the booth, Ms. Nelson walked up to Frankie.

"It looks as if you've got the most popular booth at the Spring Fair. I thought you'd be one of the dancers."

"No, ma'am," said Frankie politely. "I'm just the announcer."

"Well, good luck," said Ms. Nelson. "Those brownies that Mrs. Epstein made certainly look good. Maybe they'll give me one." She smiled. "And, maybe some cheesecake for later on!"

By two-thirty, Bunny couldn't stand looking at the toe show line any longer.

"I'm going to go over and find out what that booth's all about," Bunny said.

"Well, I wouldn't be caught dead paying my money to that stupid club," said Violetta. "It's the biggest competition we've got. And I'll die if Emily Anderson wins instead of me. Positively, absolutely die!"

"I'm going anyway," Bunny said. "I've asked at least twenty kids. And not one will tell me what the toe show is."

Just then, a shriek and a howl came from the toe show booth.

"See what I mean?" asked Bunny. "It must be pretty interesting."

"Suit yourself," said Violetta in her nastiest voice. "Just remember that if the toe show beats us by fifty cents, it will be all your fault."

CHAPTER FIVE

Nobody noticed that Bunny had her fingers crossed when she took the oath of secrecy.

"Do you want to peek or touch?" Spike asked after she finished the oath.

Bunny glanced at the price sign. "Touch," she said, plunking down three quarters quickly. She hoped Violetta wouldn't find out she'd spent even more money at the rival booth.

Bunny turned toward the inside curtain just as Jade Singer stepped out of the viewing room. Jade's freckled face was unusually pale.

"How is it?" asked Bunny.

"Creepy," Jade said, hurrying out of the booth.

"Next!" said Tulu, as she pulled aside the Star Trek curtain.

Inside the viewing room, Emily sat solemnly at the red-satin-covered desk with the black velvet box resting on top of it.

Bunny hesitated.

"Are you ready to view the toe?" Emily whispered.

"I guess," Bunny said, stepping forward. "What's the big deal?"

"The big deal is that this is my father's big toe. It got cut off in a bike accident."

"You're lying," Bunny said. "It's a fake. Probably left over from Halloween."

"No, it's for real," Emily said.

"A real cut-off toe?"

Emily raised her right hand. "Girl Scout's honor."

Bunny felt her stomach heave. "Is this a trick?" she asked, putting her hand over her mouth.

"Nope," said Emily. "Here, I'll show you."

Slowly Emily slid the inside box out of the velvet case. Then she removed the cotton. "Ta-da!" she cried as she shoved the toe right under Bunny Bigalow's nose.

Bunny squinted. She stared at the withered toe that nestled in the soft, white cotton. The rhinestones glittered and sparkled against the backdrop of black velvet and red satin.

"It *is* a toe!" Bunny shrieked. "It is!" she repeated as her stomach heaved again, her eyes fixed on the gray toenail.

Horrified, she swung her arm and accidentally knocked the toe box to the ground.

"You spilled my father's toe!" Emily howled, crawling after the toe before it rolled out of sight.

With a scream, Bunny turned to run out of the booth. But Tulu was holding the curtain down and Bunny bumped into her.

"Help!" cried Tulu, falling against the frame of the booth.

Slowly…ever so slowly…the booth began to tilt. Billy jumped up and grabbed a sheet. Spike tried to hold on to the side of the booth. But it was too late. Just before the booth crashed to the ground, Emily grabbed the toe and put it safely in the box.

"Help!" screeched Bunny as she ran right into Mr. Bottom's dalmatian. Spotty was tied to the spin art booth. And when he tried to run away, he took the booth with him.

Cans of paint tumbled and splattered all

over the ground as the spin art booth crashed into Alexander Harbottle's reptile show.

"Eeek!" screamed Mr. Yang as a giant iguana fell into his lap.

"Aaarrgh!" yelled Bunny's mother, Mrs. Bigalow, as Alexander's garter snake wrapped itself around her ankle.

A group of third graders covered with purple and pink paint ran right into the handicrafts booth. Feathers cascaded into the air and drifted overhead as the balloon booth tipped sideways. And when Sarah Blonder tried to save that booth from tipping, she let go of seventeen helium-filled balloons.

Still dragging the spin art booth behind him, Spotty collided with the popcorn popper. A volcano of popcorn erupted from the machine, scattering salty white puffs in every direction.

Spotty yelped and ran right into the ruffled, color-coordinated, periwinkle and cranberry bake sale booth.

Violetta squealed as cupcakes and cookies rolled off the table. Mrs. Epstein's cheeseless tofu cheesecake splattered all over Mr. Anderson's shoes.

"Wow!" exclaimed Spike when he looked up. Bubbles, feathers, and buttered popcorn stuck to the balloons that floated into the bright blue sky.

"Good grief," said Mr. Bottoms as he surveyed the damage.

In the midst of the commotion, Mrs. Stevens appeared, covered with green and orange paint. She ran up to where the toe show booth had been and exclaimed, "Don't tell me I'm too late to see my darling dancing girls!"

CHAPTER SIX

The shocked crowd of grown-ups and children stood quietly and looked around the playground. Alexander Harbottle carefully unwound his snake from Mrs. Bigalow's ankle, while Ms. Nelson dabbed at purple paint dripping from her skirt.

Decorated with feathers and ribbons from their handicrafts booth, two second graders fed Spotty the last of Mrs. Epstein's cheeseless tofu cheesecake. And a flock of pigeons swooped straight for the popcorn scattered all over the playground.

"What in the world happened?" asked Mr. Bottoms, shaking his head in wonder.

"I can tell you exactly what happened," said Bunny Bigalow importantly.

"It's those Canal Street kids," accused Violetta Epstein, pointing at Emily and Frankie. "It's all their fault."

Bunny poked Violetta. "Let me tell. I'm the one who saw it," she said.

"Saw what?" asked Mr. Bottoms.

Bunny shuddered. "Mr. Anderson's horrible, shriveled-up toe."

"My what?" said Mr. Anderson as he walked over to Emily.

"Your toe, Daddy," she answered. Then she took a deep breath. "The one you lost. Except it's not lost at all. I found it the day after your accident. And I have it right here."

Everybody in the playground looked at Emily's sparkling velvet box and then at Mr. Anderson's cheesecake-splattered shoes. And everybody in the playground tried to guess which foot had a missing toe.

"Why don't you start at the beginning," suggested Mr. Anderson.

Emily gulped. Here goes, she thought. Then she explained everything. When she finished, everyone was quiet. Finally Mr. Bottoms broke the silence.

"You actually displayed *a severed toe* at our

Spring Fair?" he asked.

"I thought you said it was a dance," said Mr. Yang to Ms. Nelson, but Ms. Nelson just shrugged.

"A severed toe?" Mr. Bottoms repeated.

Tulu spoke up bravely. "It was my big sister's chance to be a famous movie extra."

"Frankie's always wanted to be in the movies," added Emily.

"The toe show made *lots* of money for our school," said Frankie.

Spike raised his voice. "We thought it was a great idea."

"Something new and different," continued Billy.

"And lots of kids paid lots of money to see it," said Emily.

"It wasn't *our* fault the booth tipped over," Billy said.

"It certainly wasn't," said Emily, glaring at Bunny Bigalow.

"I think it was the most exciting Spring Fair we've ever had!" said Noah Benchley.

"Me, too!" shouted all the kids on the playground.

"What about this disgusting mess?"

Violetta reminded everyone. "They've ruined everything. Everything."

"No problem," said Ms. Nelson. "If we all get to work, this place can be cleaned up real fast."

"But the toe," protested Mr. Bottoms. "What are we going to do about Mr. Anderson's toe?"

Mr. Anderson stepped forward. "I know how you must feel, Mr. Bottoms," he said. "This *is* an unusual situation. But after all, it is *my* toe that's been on display all day. And if I don't object, I don't see why anyone else should, either."

Emily sighed with relief. "Thanks, Dad," she whispered.

Mr. Bottoms thought about it for a minute and then nodded.

Frankie looked at Mr. Anderson and began to clap loudly.

"Bravo!" called out Billy's father as he joined Frankie's applause. Soon every person on the playground was cheering and clapping. Every person except Bunny Bigalow and Violetta Epstein.

When the applause died down, Ms. Nelson spoke briskly to the crowd. "While everybody's cleaning up—and I do mean *everybody*," she said, staring at Bunny and Violetta, "Mr. Bottoms and I will count the money from the booths. We'll be able to announce the winner soon."

With the help of the grown-ups, the children cleaned the playground. In less than an hour, the job was done.

"Quiet, everybody!" said Ms. Nelson, raising her hands. "May I have your attention, please?"

Everyone gathered around Mr. Bottoms, Ms. Nelson, and Mr. Yang.

Please let us win, Emily thought. Please.

Mr. Bottoms looked at the expectant faces in the crowd and smiled his principal smile. The fake one.

"Well, well, well…" he began. He turned to Ms. Nelson. "The envelope, please," he said with a chuckle.

Ms. Nelson handed him the slip of paper with the name of the booth that had earned the most money.

"What do you suppose I have here?" he teased. Then he peeked at the paper and winked. "Now I know, and you don't."

"Ah, get on with it already," whispered Spike to Billy.

"So!" said Mr. Bottoms. "The first thing I want to tell you is that this Spring Fair raised more money than any other in the history of our school."

Everybody applauded.

Frankie rolled her eyes. "I hope this isn't one of his endless speeches," she said out of the side of her mouth.

"Spare us," whispered Emily.

"That's not the only thing that's unusual, however," continued Mr. Bottoms. "This year, for the first time, we have two winners. That's because two booths were way ahead of the others and were almost tied. It's impossible to know which one would have been the winner if the Spring Fair had gone on until three o'clock, as planned."

"Uh-oh," said Frankie, glancing at Emily. "I smell trouble."

"So," Mr. Bottoms said in his jolliest voice, "as you know, the Grand Prize winners will get to be extras in the upcoming Unicorn Films production of *Crypt Riders in the Night*."

"That doesn't sound like a dancing movie," said Mrs. Stevens doubtfully.

"And the winners are…" Mr. Bottoms

paused and cleared his throat. "The winners are...the bake sale booth and the toe show booth! Congratulations, children!"

"Hurray!" shouted Tulu.

Bunny and Violetta squealed as they jumped up and down and hugged each other.

Mr. Lopez patted Billy on the shoulder. "Way to go, son," he said proudly, while Mr. and Mrs. Anderson smiled.

The next instant, Bunny and Violetta tapped Emily on the shoulder. "You owe us each a dollar," they said as if they were Siamese twins joined at the mouth. "You didn't win."

"Neither did you," said Emily. "It was a tie. We're even. And you're not getting one penny out of me."

Bunny and Violetta sulked angrily as Emily turned to Frankie and Spike.

"We did it!" yelled Spike, making a thumbs-up sign with pride.

Frankie shook her head. "Don't you get it?" she hissed.

"Get what?" Emily asked.

Frankie's eyes flashed with irritation. "We're going to have to be in a movie with Bunny Bigalow and Violetta Epstein!"

CHAPTER SEVEN

The day after the Spring Fair, the Canal Street Club gathered for a special meeting at Emily's house. Mr. Anderson had important business to discuss with them.

"Thanks for coming," Mr. Anderson said after everybody arrived. "There's milk and cookies on the kitchen table."

When everyone was settled, Frankie looked at Mr. Anderson and said, "As club president, I want to thank you for talking to Mr. Bottoms yesterday and making everything all right."

"I was glad to help out," said Mr. Anderson. "Actually, I thought you kids were quite original." He smiled. "I admit I was a bit shocked when I heard about my toe. But after all, I've gotten used to being without it.

And I do have nine more."

All the kids gave sighs of relief. Emily smiled as she held the glittering velvet box carefully in her lap.

"The problem is," Mr. Anderson continued, "I don't think Emily should keep the toe anymore. It doesn't feel right to me. On the other hand, we don't know what to do with it. So we thought we'd ask you."

"You could donate it to medical science," offered Billy.

"I don't think my old toe would catch the imagination of a research scientist," Mr. Anderson said.

"Maybe the museum would like it," said Tulu.

"It's not old enough." Frankie shook her head. "But what about a burial at sea? We could rent a boat and everything!"

"Some fish would come along and eat it. Then it would get sick and vomit in the ocean," Spike said.

"We could bury it in your garden and plant roses on top," suggested Tulu. "That would be beautiful."

"That doesn't feel right, either," said Mr.

Anderson. "I don't need any reminders about my missing toe. All I have to do is look down."

"What about freezing it?" asked Frankie.

Mr. Anderson laughed. "As much as I wish I still had my toe, it's too late to save this one."

"Well, what do they call it when they burn bodies?" Frankie asked.

"Cremation!" answered Billy, as if he were on a vocabulary quiz show.

"We could do that," Frankie said.

Mr. Anderson looked at Emily. She smiled at her father. "Yes. We *could* do that," said Mr. Anderson.

CHAPTER EIGHT

That evening, the kids stood outside and watched in silence as Mr. Anderson fanned the charcoal in the grill.

"Ready?" he asked Emily.

"Yes," she said solemnly. Then she nodded at Billy Lopez, who stepped forward.

"Billy's composed a poem for the occasion," Emily said to her father.

"It's called a eulogy," corrected Frankie.

Mr. Anderson nodded. "Thank you, Billy," he said. "That's very thoughtful of you."

Billy cleared his throat. He took a piece of paper from his pocket and began.

"Farewell, farewell, O noble Toe.
Thanks for starring in our show.

We'll light your fire and say good-bye,
But as the stars light up the sky,

We wish you may, we wish you might
Find a foot that fits just right."

Without a word, Emily opened the velvet-covered matchbox and dropped the toe into the blazing fire.

Then Mr. Anderson placed the cover over the grill. "That's it, kids. Thanks for coming, everybody," he said, his arm around Emily.

The next evening, Emily tiptoed into her room and hid a large bag of ashes under her bed.

Wait till next year, she thought. Just wait.

About the Authors

Nancy Lamb was born and raised in Oklahoma. She is the author of *The Great Mosquito, Bull and Coffin Caper,* and under the pseudonym of R.G. Austin has co-authored twelve *Which Way* books and thirteen *Which Way/Secret Door* books with Rita Gelman. Ms. Lamb lives in Venice, California.

Muff Singer is the author of *What Does Kitty See?*, *Little Lamb Lost,* and *Hello Piglet.* This is her second book in collaboration with Nancy Lamb, who is her neighbor in Venice, California.

You won't want to miss the next
CANAL STREET KIDS BOOK

The Vampires Went Thataway!

by Nancy Lamb and Muff Singer
illustrated by Blanche Sims

The Canal Street Kids are up to their old tricks—and some new ones, too. After tying for the first-place prize of movie extras, the five club members are stuck on the film set of a vampire western with their longtime rivals, Bunny Bigalow and Violetta Epstein.

But the movie set isn't the only place where vampires are lurking. Spike Piranna is sure that Violetta is a vampire, too—and he's got proof! An evening encounter in a cemetery sets the stage for mischief and laughter in this second Canal Street Kids book.

0-8167-3718-5 $2.95 U.S. / $3.95 CAN.

Available wherever you buy books.

little rainbow®

Look for these other books from

little rainbow®

THE BIRTHDAY WISH MYSTERY
by Faye Couch Reeves
illustrated by Marilyn Mets
0-8167-3531-X $2.95 U.S. / $3.95 Can.

MICE TO THE RESCUE
by Michelle V. Dionetti
illustrated by Carol Newsom
0-8167-3515-8 $2.50 U.S. / $3.50 Can.

THREE DOLLAR MULE
by Clyde Robert Bulla
illustrated by Paul Lantz
0-8167-3598-0 $2.50 U.S. / $3.50 Can.

CAITLIN'S BIG IDEA
by Gloria Skurzynski
illustrated by Cathy Diefendorf
0-8167-3592-1 $2.50 U.S. / $3.50 Can.

NORMAN NEWMAN:
MY SISTER THE WITCH
by Ellen Conford
illustrated by Tim Jacobus
0-8167-3623-5 $2.50 U.S. / $3.50 Can.

Available wherever you buy books.